S0-EIH-615

Cheating Chet

Published by MM&I Ink, Bayard, NE 69334

To Order Extra Copies:
Monte R. RR1, Box 432, Bayard, NE 69334
Don D. P.O. Box 2578 Olathe KS 66062
HPP P.O. Box 444, Minatare, NE 69356

$3.00 Single Copy + 50¢ Postage
Dealer/Teacher inquires Welcome
Contact for Volume rates!

Copyright 1991 Monte Reichenberg
Illustrations Copyright 1991 Don Dane
Printed by High Plains Printing, Minatare, NE 69356
All rights Reserved
Library of Congress registration No. Applied for.

Author, Monte Reichenberg, believes that learning should be fun.

CHEATING CHET was written not only to provide enjoyable reading and coloring, but also to give students a fun, easy way to learn about long and short "E" sounds.

Monte has used **CHEATING CHET** and the soon to be released, **SAM, OLD KATE AND I** for all the school residenceies that he has conducted for the Nebraska Arts Council as an Artist in the Schools/Communities since the spring of 1991.

Both stories were so well accepted by students and teachers from all grade levels that Monte decided to publish the stories as coloring books.

DON DANE ©1992

MONTE TELLS THE STORIES WHILE DON DRAWS THEM!

HOW THIS BOOK CAME TO BE

Monte Reichenberg was working his summer job as a guide at the Oregon Trail Wagon Train near Bayard, Nebraska, when a guest came up and asked to take Monte's picture.

A conversation resulted and Monte found out that the guest, Don Dane, of Olathe, Kansas, was an artist.

Monte told Don about a children's story he had written and asked Don if he would be willing to do the illustrations for it.

Don said he had never illustrated a book before, but he would be willing to try.

The result of that chance meeting is the illustrated story and coloring book entitled "CHEATING CHET".

Cheating 'Chet was known to steal.
He was involved in many a raw deal.

Chet lived next door to Hard-hearing Ed.
Chet thought Ed was soft in the head,

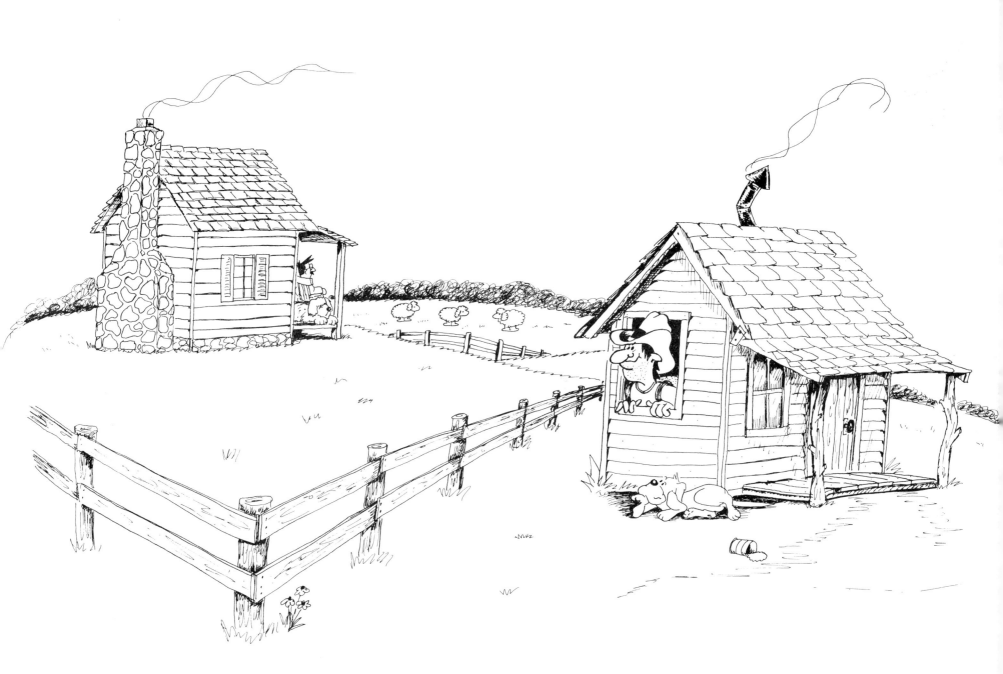

but Ed was as smart as any of his peers.
He'd just never cleaned the wax from his ears.
Hard hearing Ed raised lots of sheep,
tried to keep them safe 'cause sheep are not cheap.

But Ed slept with his head twixt pillow and sheet.
He couldn't even hear his frightened sheep bleat.

Chet had a dog named Pete for a pet,
Pete had to steal for that cheating Chet.

Of what he wanted, Chet would
draw a sketch,
then he'd send out Pete, who had
to go fetch.

Pete wasn't happy 'bout this thieving scene,
but if he didn't go, Chet would get mean.

Late one night after Ed went to
sleep,
Chet and Pete tried to steal away
his sheep.
But hardhearing Ed had a pet
named Shep,
an eye on the sheep, Shep always
kept,
he'd pretend that he was fast
asleep,
making sure to watch for a thieving creep.

Chet told Pete to creep among the sheep,
and prepare to leap while Shep was asleep.
At pretending sleep, Shep was quite adept.
He did not sleep but watched Pete as he crept.

Pete found a sheep upon which to leap,
but before he could leap at the sleeping sheep,
up leaped Shep from where he'd supposedly slept.
When up leaped Shep, Pete could have wept,

but before Pete could let out a
peep,
he was in a fight amidst of the
sheep.
Now Pete was little, wiry and lean,
while Shep was big, hairy and
mean.

In no time at all, Pete could easy see,
easy see,
there was some place else that he'd rather be.
he'd rather be.
Away from the scene of his foul deed,
deed,
Pete tried to flee at a high rate of speed,
speed,

But Shep wasn't through and after
Pete, Shep sped
figuring to put knots on top of
Pete's head.
Pete on his feet was really quite
fleet,
he looked over his shoulder as he
made his retreat.
What he saw was enough to make
him scream,
Shep was right there like a mons-
ter in a dream.

Shep was very good at beating feet,
he stayed on the heels of the flee-ing Pete,
and every time Shep would draw near,
he'd take a big bite out of Pete's running rear.
Pete was getting a little upset,
his life of crime, he was starting to regret.

He turned a corner and there stood Chet.

It was a sight Chet'll never forget, saw his pet get a wound in his seat.

It was just too much for the flee-ing Pete.

He wanted revenge you can just bet.
Pete started chasing that Cheating Chet.
Pete was after Chet and Shep was after Pete,
they made lots of noise racing up the street.

The last time we looked they were headed west,
if they never come back it's probably best.
Far as we know they're running yet,
Shep behind Pete and Pete behind Cheating Chet.